For Karen and Brian
—L.J.

For David and Jane
—C.W.

Text copyright © 1996 by Linda Jennings
Illustrations copyright © 1996 by Catherine Walters

CIP Data is available.

Published in the United States 1996
by Dutton Children's Books,
a division of Penguin Books USA Inc.
375 Hudson Street, New York, New York 10014
Originally published in Great Britain 1996 by
Magi Publications, London
Typography by Julia Goodman
Printed in Belgium
First American Edition
ISBN 0-525-45692-9
1 3 5 7 9 10 8 6 4 2

The Best Christmas Present of All

by **Linda Jennings**

illustrated by **Catherine Walters**

DUTTON CHILDREN'S BOOKS   New York

$\mathcal{B}$uster was a small dog with a black patch over one eye. He lived with Mr. Merriweather, who had taken him in when he was a stray. Buster loved his owner and their snug home. And when Mr. Merriweather's grandchildren came to visit, they would all go for long walks in the park together. Jake, Becky, and Rose would run with Buster and give him lots of treats.

One day, when Jake got out Buster's leash as usual, Mr. Merriweather shook his head.

"Sorry, children," he said. "I'm not feeling well. Take Buster out in the yard instead."

After that, Mr. Merriweather took Buster only for short walks, but Buster didn't mind. He was happy enough just living quietly at home with his friend.

Then everything changed. One morning Mr. Merriweather did not come downstairs for breakfast. Buster
whined and scratched at the kitchen door. Though he
could hear Mr. Merriweather's faint voice from upstairs,
the old man did not come down.

Later that morning, Mr. Merriweather's daughter, Mary,
arrived. As she gave Buster his breakfast, a big, white van
with a red cross on it pulled up in front of the house.

Buster saw Mr. Merriweather being carried downstairs on a stretcher. He reached over to pet Buster, but before the little dog could lick his hand, Mr. Merriweather was taken outside to the white van.

"It will be okay, Buster," Mary said as she fastened his leash and walked him out to the car. But Buster pulled away. He was frightened and confused. Once, long ago, some people had put him in a car and driven to a strange part of town, where they left him all alone.

Mary picked up Buster and put him on the backseat. Buster looked sadly out the window at his home as they drove away. Where had Mr. Merriweather gone?

At last the car swung into a driveway, and Mary opened the back door.

"It's Buster!" the children shouted as they rushed out of the house.

"Grandpa has had a heart attack," said Mary. "He'll be in the hospital for a while, so we're going to take care of Buster."

The children looked sad, but they petted Buster and offered him a cookie.

"Can we take him for a walk?" asked Rose, tugging at his leash.

But Buster was still scared. The children were making so much noise that he wanted to get away from them and go back to Mr. Merriweather.

Buster wriggled and pulled until his collar came off. Then, before anyone could stop him, he ran down the driveway and into the street. Buster was going home.

But this part of town was unfamiliar to him. And some of the shoppers rushing along the sidewalks bumped into the little dog. A few people even yelled at him as he ran by. Their angry voices reminded Buster of the time when he was a stray. No one shouted at him when he was with Mr. Merriweather.

At long last he came to the very park where Mr. Merriweather and the children had taken him for walks. He dashed through the playground and down to the pond, just in case Mr. Merriweather was there on his favorite bench. But he wasn't.

Buster sat down and hung his head. Suddenly, a big dog ran up to him. He sniffed Buster and began to growl.

"Get lost, mutt," he barked as he chased Buster to the edge of the park, before racing off again.

Buster had to stop and rest. So much had happened to him that day, and he was tired and hungry. But there, right ahead, was his home! He ran up to it happily. The front gate was shut, so he jumped right over the wall.

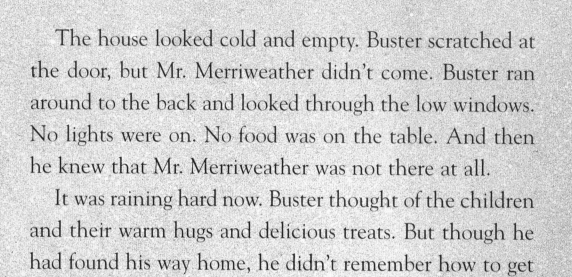

The house looked cold and empty. Buster scratched at the door, but Mr. Merriweather didn't come. Buster ran around to the back and looked through the low windows. No lights were on. No food was on the table. And then he knew that Mr. Merriweather was not there at all.

It was raining hard now. Buster thought of the children and their warm hugs and delicious treats. But though he had found his way home, he didn't remember how to get back to them. He was lost again.

A car pulled up in front of the house. Buster ran into the bushes to hide.

"Buster! Buster!" called three worried voices. "Are you there, Buster?"

It was the children!

Buster crawled out, his stumpy tail wagging for the first time that day. Jake picked him up and hugged him. Buster felt warm in his arms.

"You're coming home with us, Buster," cried Rose. And all the way back in the car, she fed Buster treat after treat and stroked his wet fur.

Buster never ran away again, though he still missed his old friend. Then one special winter day, Buster had a surprise. . . .

The front door opened, and there he was!

"I've missed you, Buster!" Mr. Merriweather whispered, hugging the little dog tightly.

"Grandpa's coming to live with us," said Becky. "Won't that be great!"

Buster wagged his tail and licked Mr. Merriweather's face. This was the best Christmas present of all.